The Tortoise and the Hare

A Tale about Determination

Retold by Joanne Barkan
Illustrated by Susan Jaekel

Famous Fables™

Reader's Digest Young Families

One fine summer day, a tortoise, a lizard, a squirrel, a skunk, and a raccoon gathered at their favorite spot by the side of a pond.

Tortoise and Lizard sunned themselves on a large rock. Raccoon cleaned her paws. Squirrel and Skunk watched fluffy white clouds drift across the sky.

Everything was calm and peaceful, and then—

Hare leaped out of the bushes!

"Up, up, up, lazy ones," he called out. "You're wasting a beautiful day. Let's do something fun. Let's have a race around the pond!"

Squirrel sighed and said, "You always want to race because you think you're faster than everyone else."

"Think?" Hare shouted. "I *am* the fastest! I can run circles around all of you! No one can beat me!"

Hare bragged on and on, and all the while, he thumped his long feet on the ground.

"Good-bye peace and quiet," Skunk grumbled.

"This is no fun at all," Squirrel complained.

"He's ruining our day," Raccoon groaned.

Tortoise raised her head and said quietly, "I'll race you, Hare."

For a moment, all the animals were silent.

Then Hare began to shout, "Tortoise wants to race me? That's an insult! You're the slowest animal I've ever met! It will take you hours to get around the pond!"

The other animals were puzzled. How could Tortoise even think of racing Hare? they wondered.

Tortoise just climbed down from her rock and slowly walked to the path that went around the pond. When she reached it, she said, "I'm ready."

"Tortoise, I will not race you," insisted Hare.

"Are you afraid of losing?" Tortoise asked.

"Afraid of losing!" Hare laughed at the thought.

All the other animals were now waiting near the path. They were watching Hare. Finally he stomped over and stood next to Tortoise.

"Okay," Tortoise said, "let's make this the starting
line. I'll show all of you what fast really means."
Lizard spoke up in her high-pitched voice.
"Attention, racers! On your mark...get set...go!"

Hare sprang into the air. His strong hind legs moved him forward in huge leaps. He charged up the path, saying to himself, "Faster! Faster! Faster!" After a minute or two, he glanced back to see where Tortoise was.

"I knew this would happen," Hare said. "Tortoise is barely across the starting line!"

Hare took a few more leaps and then stopped. "This is ridiculous!" he muttered. "It's going to take Tortoise the rest of the afternoon to get around the pond. I might as well take a little nap. When I wake up, I'll still be able to run around the pond ten times before she gets around it once."

Hare stretched out along the side of the path. He arranged his long ears in a comfortable position. He yawned and closed his eyes. Soon he was snoring.

Z-z-z-z. Z-z-z-z. Z-z—

Hare awoke with a start. He sat up quickly and looked around. His mouth dropped open in surprise. "The sun!" he said. "It's so low in the sky!"

Then Hare heard far-off voices shouting. He jumped up and started running as fast as he could. He ran and ran until he saw his friends in the distance. They were jumping up and down. They were cheering. Tortoise was crossing the finish line!

When Hare reached his friends, they were standing around Tortoise and clapping.

"Aren't you going to congratulate Tortoise on winning the race?" Raccoon asked.

Hare mumbled, "Congratulations, Tortoise." Then he groaned and said, "How could this happen?"

"Well," Tortoise replied, "slow and steady wins the race." She turned, climbed onto her rock, and quietly watched the beautiful sunset.

Famous Fables, Lasting Virtues
Tips for Parents

Now that you've read The Tortoise and the Hare, *use these pages as a guide to teach your child the virtues in the story. By talking about the story and its message and engaging in the suggested activities, you can help your child develop good judgment and a strong moral character.*

About Determination

Learning to work toward a goal "slowly and steadily" without getting distracted is something even young children can do. Young children often set goals for themselves without even realizing it—for example, completing a drawing or building a tower with tiny blocks. And often children don't—or won't—stop until they have finished their task! Longer-term goals are a bit more frustrating for children because of the time it takes to reach them. Here are some ideas to help you instill in your child the kind of determination demonstrated by Tortoise in the story.

1. *Share your own goals.* Talk about your own goals with your children. You may be saving for their college education or for a new car. You may want to take up an old pastime, such as playing an instrument, or learn something new, such as teaching yourself how to refinish furniture. Or you may want to clean out the attic or the garage! Share your small setbacks and triumphs with your children so they can see determination being modeled by a powerful role model—you.

2. *Practice makes perfect.* Often young children look at an accomplished or well-known athlete and wonder why they are unable to do what the athlete can. Talk to your children about how the athlete has worked very hard, practicing every day, to attain that level of accomplishment.

3. *Set attainable goals.* Write down some age-appropriate goals for your child, such as learning to tie a bow, making pancake batter, or riding a two-wheeler. Once your child has accomplished early successes, she should be more willing to apply her work ethic toward such things as homework, sports, or a musical instrument.